WAYNE ANDERSON

HORRORBLE BOOK

Come into the graveyard, where all is deadly still.

No ghost, no gremlin, no ghoul, no goblin,
nobody stirs.

Suddenly the ground opens with
a thunderous crack.
"Who's there?" you shout into
the gaping earth.

"*No Body!*" comes the unearthly reply.
And out of the black hole slithers a
creature that truly has no body, just
a head and arms and some bits and
pieces it has stolen from the graves.

The creature vanishes into the nearby forest. Soon there is the sound of someone chopping wood. **"Who's there?"** you shout into the night shadows.

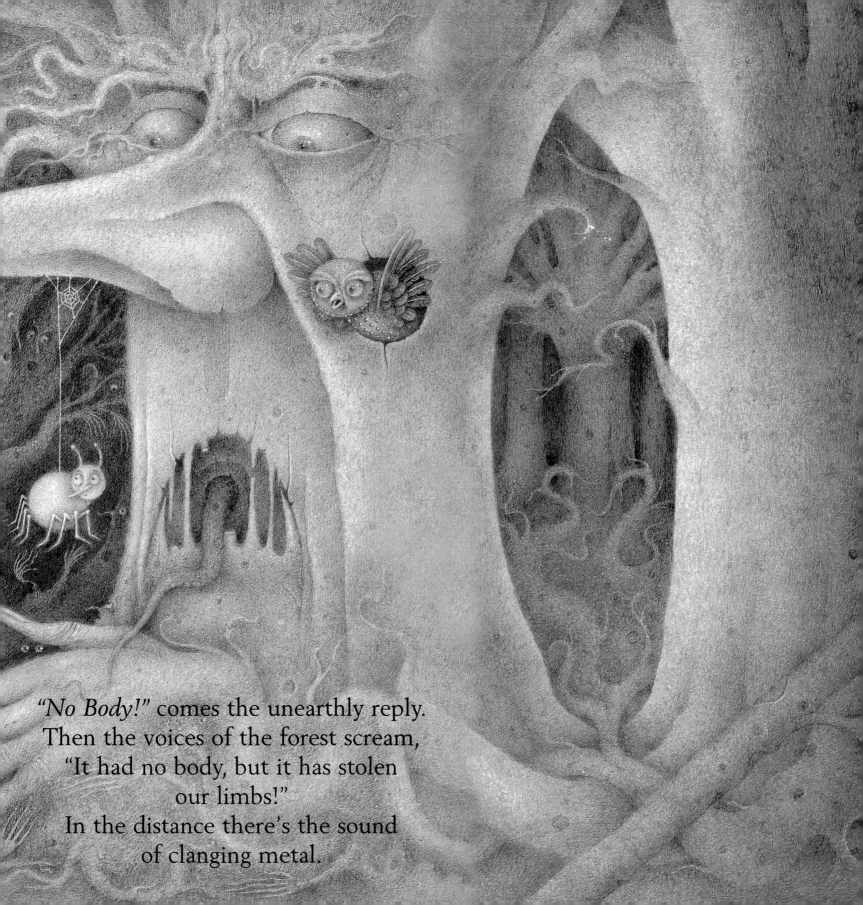

"No Body!" comes the unearthly reply.
Then the voices of the forest scream,
"It had no body, but it has stolen
our limbs!"
In the distance there's the sound
of clanging metal.

You follow the noise to the swamp.
"Who's there?" you shout into
the watery world.

"*No Body!*" comes the unearthly reply.
Then all the underwater creatures
bubble, "It had no body, but it has
made off with our fins and skins,
our scales and tails!"

Finally, you come to a cave. All is silent. Have you imagined everything? You shout, **"Is anybody there?"**

"Not just Any Body,"
comes the distant reply.
Then the cave echoes with
squeaks and shrieks, "It has wood
and metal, fins and skin, and bits
and pieces from the graveyard.
It's building itself a real body...."

From far inside the deepest tunnel
of the cave, infernal noises grow
louder as you move closer.
"Is somebody there?" you shout.
"Yes," comes the all too earthly reply.

"Some Body is here and ready to meet you...."

The funny thing was, the next time Herb's mother came to read the
wolf story, there was no wolf to be seen – just a tiny caterpillar
trying with all his might to terrify a little girl in a red coat.

Then he switched off his light aND DREAMED of Fierce CATERPILLARS fashionable wolves and grouchy godmothers

Before Herb got back into bed he piled
up all his books and then put the
heaviest thing he could find on top of
them, just in case anyone else was
tempted to get out of his story.

'Oh, I do like caterpillars,' said the Fairy Godmother, popping it back in to the wolf storybook. 'They're so undemanding. Never bothering me for things, not like frogs, always thinking they are princes. What's more, I really have had enough of being squashed inside a book, doing favours for spoilt princesses. I'm going to take a holiday, somewhere far away from royalty.'

And in a sudden twinkle of sequins, she disappeared.

Quick as a quick thing the Fairy Godmother whooshed her wand
and Big Wolf was just a tiny caterpillar.

'Help!'

screeched Herb.

The Fairy Godmother was
so engrossed with her own
problems that she hadn't
noticed that Big Wolf
was poised, ready
to swallow Herb
in one gulp.

'Oh well, that's that then,'
sighed the Fairy Godmother.
'I'm not going to be at all
popular at the palace now.
I don't know what the
king and queen are going
to say when a wolf
turns up at the ball
to dance with their
son. I imagine
they will be very
grumpy about it.
I do hope he
doesn't start
snacking on
the guests . . .'

Which of course left Cinderella having a night in,
cleaning the kitchen after all.

Little Wolf
took one look in
the mirror and was
so pleased with his
new look that he
jumped into the
fairy-tale book and
went to the ball
himself.

As she said this she accidentally waved her wand at the little wolf and the smoke went poof (just like in the fairy tales) and suddenly there was the little wolf standing in a ballgown.

'Oh dear, oh dear, this will never do,' said the Fairy Godmother, shaking her head. 'That dress was meant for Cinderella. You shook me out of the book just as I was about to send her to the ball. Awfully nice dress though. I have an eye for fashion as you can probably tell. But not at all suitable for a wolf.'

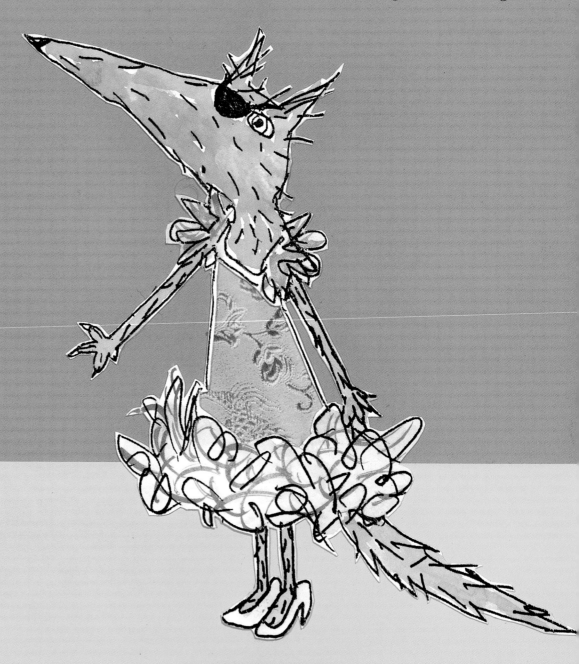

'No, no!' said Herb. 'Don't turn me into a caterpillar;
it's those two who need to be caterpillars.'
'Oh no, not you two again,' said the Godmother,
spying the two alarmed wolves. 'Always making
trouble... blowing people's houses
down and gobbling them up
without so much as a do-you-mind?'

Herb could tell things had taken a turn for the really quite bad. So he snatched up the fairy-tale book, found the page with the *Fairy Godmother* and shook it until she tumbled out of the book and on to the floor. She was a bit cross actually because her dress got crumpled and she nearly twisted her ankle. 'Well,' she said, 'I've got a good mind to turn you into a caterpillar, little boy.'

'Oh, you dozy doormats, don't you know anything?' snarled the fairy. 'You wolf-half-wits give wickedness a bad name. He's tricked you, you twerps: little boys are starters, jelly is pudding.'

And with that the wicked fairy jumped back into the book and snapped it shut.

First the wolves went almost purple in the cheeks with embarrassment, then their eyes went all mean and squinty.

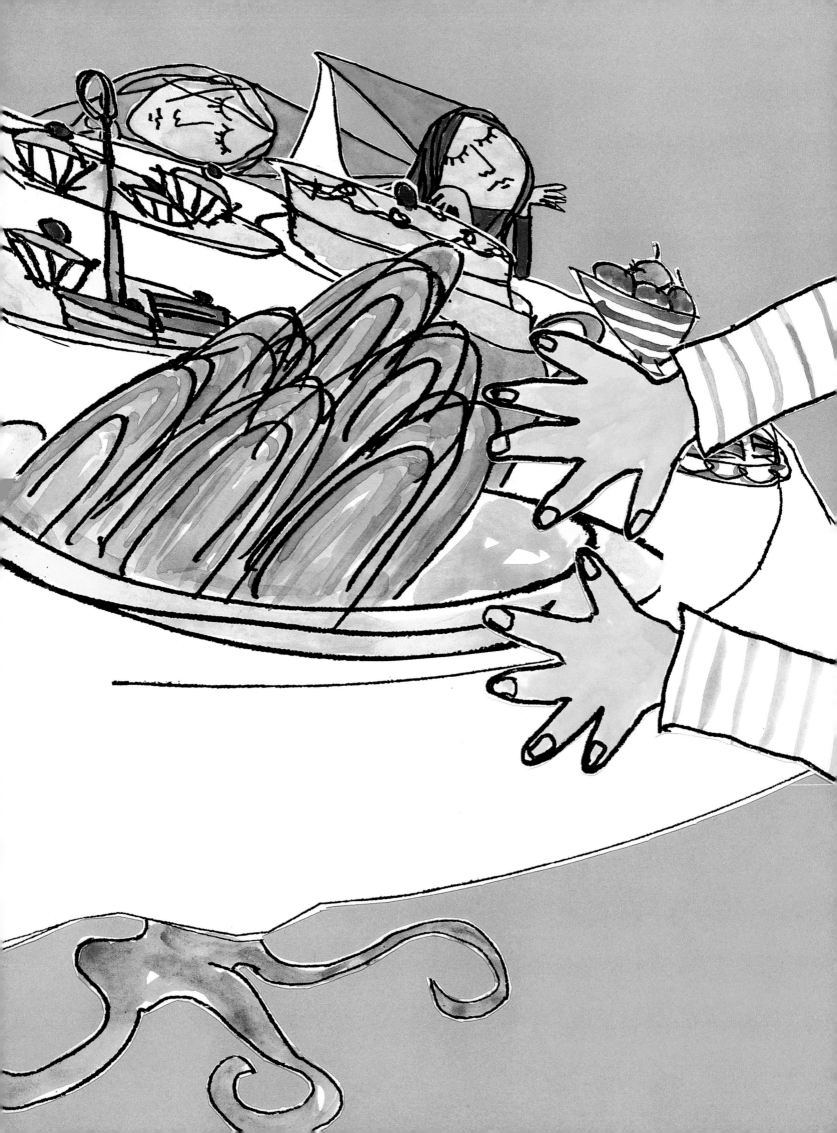

Herb was so busy struggling to slide the jelly off the page he didn't notice the wicked fairy, wide awake and hiding under the table. She had been listening to every word.

This was bad luck for Herb because the wicked fairy hated little boys only slightly less than she hated little girls. They made her very nervous. She'd seen what those little brats, Hansel and Gretel, had done to that poor defenceless witch. Not only did they nibble her cottage half to pieces, but then they went and shoved her in her own oven. Children put her in a very bad mood indeed.

No one at the table would notice if he borrowed a jelly. They were all snoozing, tired of waiting for *Princess Beautiful* to wake up.

You could tell that Little Wolf hadn't even heard of starters but, not wishing to sound stupid, he shouted, 'Jelly is starters! Everybody knows that.'

Then Big Wolf and Little Wolf looked at Herb and said, 'Where's the jelly?'

Jelly, jelly, where was a jelly?

Herb's mind was whirring like a frantic thing.

Then he caught sight of his book of fairy tales.

He had been looking at it last night and it was lying open on the page where the dozy princess falls asleep at her own birthday party.

'Ummm ... because little boys are
for pudding. You have to start
with starters, of course.'
'I didn't know that,' said Big Wolf.
'Really?' said Herb, feeling a little bit
pleased with his own craftiness.
'I thought everybody knew that.'
'Oh, I knew that,' said Little Wolf.
'No, you did not,' said Big
Slightly-less-fierce-than-before Wolf.
'Yes, I certainly did,' said
Little Wolf, puffing himself up.
'Well, if you're so clever
then what's 'starters'?'
triumphed Big Wolf.

'I wouldn't eat me yet,' stammered
Herb, desperately trying to think
of a plan to distract the wolves
from wolfing him.
'**Why not?**' said Big Wolf, giving
him a sideways stare.
'**Yes, why not?**' said Little Wolf,
trying to give him a sideways stare.

And he tried to lick his chops,
but he wasn't very good at it and just
ended up dribbling on the carpet.

...and there, standing in front of him, was the **big storybook wolf** and next to him was the other **smaller wolf** with a patch over one eye (Herb recognised him as the back-cover wolf).

'Mmm,' Big Wolf said in a low greedy voice, **'I thought I could smell something tasty. I'm going to gobble you up, little boy.'** And he started to lick his chops.

'Ooh, can I have his little pink toes? They look just like piglets,' said Little Wolf.

It was like the
rumbling of a
very hungry
tummy. Or
perhaps even
two very
hungry
tummies.

Then he began
to smell a not-
very-nice smell.
A sort of bad-
breath type of a
smell. Herb got
a funny feeling
that two, or
maybe even
three, eyes were
watching him.

Unwisely, he
switched on
the light . . .

Little Red
Riding Hood

One night, just as they were finishing the
wolf story, the telephone rang.
In her hurry, Herb's mother forgot all
about taking the book with her.

Herb didn't
realise at first
but, as he was
snoozing off, he
thought he
heard a deep
rumbling sound
coming from his
bedside table.

Whenever his mother finished
this bedtime story, Herb would
say, 'Don't forget to take that
book with you!'
And his mother would ask, 'Why?'
'Because there's a wolf in it,
of course,' Herb would say.

Herb's mother would smile
to herself because she knew
that storybook wolves are not
at all dangerous.

...it had all turned out well and went happy-ever-afterly.

It was one of Herb's favourites. He particularly liked the back cover that had a picture of a smaller wolf with a patch over one eye and the words:

For a real thrill try reading the story of

THE LITTLE FIERCE WOLF

AND THE THREE PINK PIGLETS

It will scare your socks off.

Every night Herb's mother would read him a bedtime story. Sometimes it was about a big wolf who terrified little girls and their grandmothers with his chilling growl and his big yellow teeth. You could tell from the picture that toothpaste had never been on his shopping list.

The story got very nasty in the middle and everybody nearly came to a sticky end ... but, by the last page ...

For Charlie
(make sure you keep this book under something heavy)

and Cress
(who knows how to deal with storybook wolves)

Thank you to Soren

Written and illustrated by Lauren Child
British Library Cataloguing
in Publication Data
A catalogue record of this
book is available
from the British Library

ISBN 0 340 77915 2 (HB)
ISBN 0 340 77916 0 (PB)

Copyright © Lauren Child 2000

The right of Lauren Child to be identified as author and
illustrator of this Work has been asserted by her in accordance
with the Copyright, Designs and Patents Act 1988.

First edition published 2000

10 9 8 7 6 5 4 3 2 1

Published by Hodder Children's Books,
a division of Hodder Headline Limited,
338 Euston Road, London NW1 3BH

Printed in Hong Kong
All rights reserved

Little Red
Riding Hood

Beware of
the Storybook
Wolves

Lauren Child

*Hodder
Children's
Books*

A division of Hodder Headline Limited